Dear Parent:
Your child's love of reading starts here!

Every child learns to read in a different way and at his or her own speed. You can help your young reader improve and become more confident by encouraging his or her own interests and skills. You can also guide your child's spiritual development by introducing basic values and Bible stories, like I Can Read! books for every stage of reading. From books your child reads with you to the books he or she reads alone, there are I Can Read! books for every stage of reading:

SHARED READING

My First

Basic language, word repetition, and whimsical illustrations, ideal for sharing with your emergent reader.

BEGINNING READING

Short sentences, familiar words, and simple concepts for children eager to read on their own.

READING WITH HELP

Engaging stories, longer sentences, and language play for developing readers.

READING ALONE

Complex plots, challenging vocabulary, and high-interest topics for the independent reader.

ADVANCED READING

Short paragraphs, chapters, and exciting themes for the perfect bridge to chapter books.

I Can Read! books have introduced children to the joy of reading since 1957. Featuring award-winning authors and illustrators and a fabulous cast of beloved characters, I Can Read! books set the standard for beginning readers.

A lifetime of discovery begins with the magical words *"I Can Read!"*

Visit www.icanread.com for information on enriching your child's reading experience.
Visit www.zonderkidz.com for more Zonderkidz I Can Read! titles.

He who watches over you won't get tired.

—Psalm 121:3

The children's group
of Zondervan

www.zonderkidz.com

Jake's Brave Night
Copyright © 2007 by Crystal Bowman
Illustrations © 2007 by Karen Maizel
Originally published in *Jonathan James Says, "I Can Be Brave"* © 1995
ISBN-10: 0-310-71456-7
ISBN-13: 978-0-310-71456-9

Requests for information should be addressed to:
Grand Rapids, Michigan 49530

Library of Congress Cataloging-in-Publication Data

Bowman, Crystal.
    Jake's brave night / story by Crystal Bowman ; pictures by Karen Maizel.
        p. cm. – (Jake's Biblical values series) (I can read! Level 2)
        Summary: At first Jake is afraid to sleep all alone in his new room,
but when he learns that God is always with him and never sleeps,
he feels much better.
    ISBN-13: 978-0-310-71456-9 (softcover)
    ISBN-10: 0-310-71456-7 (softcover)
    [1. Fear–Fiction. 2. Bedtime–Fiction. 3. Christian life–Fiction.]
I. Maizel, Karen, ill. II. Title.
PZ7.B68335Jak 2007
[E]–dc22
                                                        2006029334

Zonderkidz is a trademark of Zondervan.

Art Direction: Laura Maitner-Mason
Cover and Interior Design: Jody Langley

Printed in China

07 08 09 10 11 • 10 9 8 7 6 5 4 3 2 1

zonder**kidz** **I Can Read!**™ READING WITH HELP 2

Jake's Brave Night

story by Crystal Bowman

pictures by Karen Maizel

"Time for bed, Jake," said Mother.

Jake brushed his teeth

and put on his pajamas.

He was excited to go to bed!

Jake was going to sleep

in his very own bedroom.

He always shared a bedroom

with his little sister, Kelly.

But not anymore.

Jake was growing up.

It was time for his own room.

Jake snuggled under the covers.

Father read him a Bible story.

Mother prayed with Jake

and gave him a kiss.

"Good night, Jake," they said.

"Good night," Jake replied.

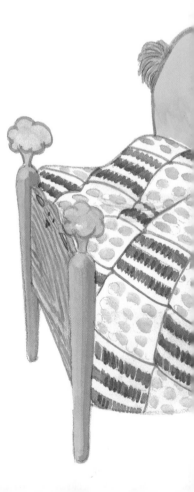

Jake closed his eyes.

Soon he opened his eyes.

He could not fall asleep.

It was very dark in his room.

He did not like the dark.

"I will turn on the light

so it won't be dark," he thought.

Jake climbed out of bed.

He turned on the light.

"That is much better!"

Jake crawled back into bed.

He looked around his bedroom.

The animals on his dresser

made scary shadows on the wall.

He did not like the shadows.

Jake climbed out of bed.

He turned out the light.

He crawled back into bed.

Then he closed his eyes.

Soon he opened his eyes.

He could not fall asleep.

He did not like being all alone.

"I will snuggle with my animals,"

thought Jake.

"Then I will not be alone."

Jake climbed out of bed.

He took the animals off his dresser

and put them in his bed.

Jake crawled into bed.

It was too crowded.

His fuzzy brown monkey

tickled his nose—Ah-choo!

Jake put the animals

back on the dresser.

He did not crawl back into bed.

Jake crawled under his bed.

Then he closed his eyes.

Soon he opened his eyes.

He could not fall asleep.

The floor was too hard.

Jake was cold.

Jake was very tired.

He crawled into bed one more time.

He closed his eyes one more time

and finally fell asleep.

Soon it was time for breakfast.

"Good morning, Jake,"

said Mother.

"You look tired," said Father.

"I did not sleep well,"

Jake told them.

"Why not?" asked Father.

"It was dark," said Jake.

"I was afraid."

"What an awful night!" said Mother.

"We will get you a night light,"
said Father.

"But I will still be all alone,"
Jake replied.

"You are never alone," said Mother.

"God is always with you."

"But when does he go to sleep?"
Jake asked.

"God never sleeps," said Father.

"God stays awake all the time."

"That is nice to know," said Jake.

He drank his orange juice

and ate his blueberry pancake.

That night, Jake brushed his teeth
and put on his pajamas.
Father read him a Bible story.
Mother prayed with Jake
and gave him a kiss.
"Good night, Jake," they said.
"Good night," said Jake.

Jake snuggled under the covers.

He did not turn on the light.

He did not take his animals to bed.

He did not crawl under his bed.

"God is watching me all night long,"

thought Jake.

Then he closed his eyes
and fell asleep.